P9-DIF-527

Minor Incidents
and
Absolute Uncertainties

ALSO BY BOOKI VIVAT

FRAZZLED

Everyday Disasters and Impending Doom

FRAZZLED

Ordinary Mishaps and Inevitable Catastrophes

BOOKI VIVAT

FRAZZLED

MINOR INCIDENTS
and
absolute
UNCERTAINTIES

HARPER

An Imprint of Harper Collins*Publishers*

 For information address HarperCollins Children's Books, a division of HarperCollins Publishers, 195 Broadway, New York, NY 10007.
www.harpercollinschildrens.com

Names: Vivat, Booki, author, illustrator.
Title: Minor incidents and absolute uncertainties / Booki Vivat.
Description: First edition. | New York, NY: Harper, an imprint of HarperCollins Publishers, [2019] | Summary: When Abbie Wu goes to "OutdoorSchool," with her older brother as a counselor, she is torn between excitement and anxiety but decides to make it a life-changing adventure.
Identifiers: LCCN 2018025426 | ISBN 9780062398833 (hardback)
Subjects: | CYAC: School field trips--Fiction. | Camps--Fiction. | Middle schools--Fiction. | Schools--Fiction. | Brothers and sisters--Fiction. | Anxiety--Fiction. | BISAC: JUVENILE FICTION / Social Issues / Self-Esteem & Self-Reliance. | JUVENILE FICTION / School & Education.
Classification: LCC PZ7.1.V69 Min 2019 | DDC [Fic]--dc23 LC record available at https://lccn.loc.gov/2018025426

---

18 19 20 21 22 CG/LSCH 10 9 8 7 6 5 4 3 2 1

❖

First Edition

For all the friends who make life feel
a little less frazzled

Minor Incidents
and
Absolute Uncertainties

CHAPTER ONE

I never thought I'd say it, but I was starting to get used to life in middle school.

DON'T GET ME WRONG.

I still thought the Middles were the worst, but I had survived so far and there were things about middle school that I knew I could expect . . .

like which routes to take to avoid the Spencer sisters,

when to talk
to teachers,

(at least fifteen
minutes after coffee)

how fast I needed to walk
to class so I wasn't tardy,

and who to eat lunch
with every day.

But when we started hearing rumblings of something different:

I didn't know WHAT to expect.

Vice Principal Kline tried to make our class trip sound all official by calling it an

ANNUAL OUTDOOR EXPLORATION AND ENVIRONMENTAL EDUCATION SUMMIT

But everybody else just called it

I had heard about Outdoor School from Peter, but I generally made it a point to be skeptical of things that Peter liked.

Plus, Nature and I had a history of not always getting along.

I even had this recurring nightmare of getting lost in the woods, choosing the wrong path, and facing some kind of gruesome end.

But everyone else seemed excited to go, and the more they talked about it, the more it sounded . . .

SNACK SHACK

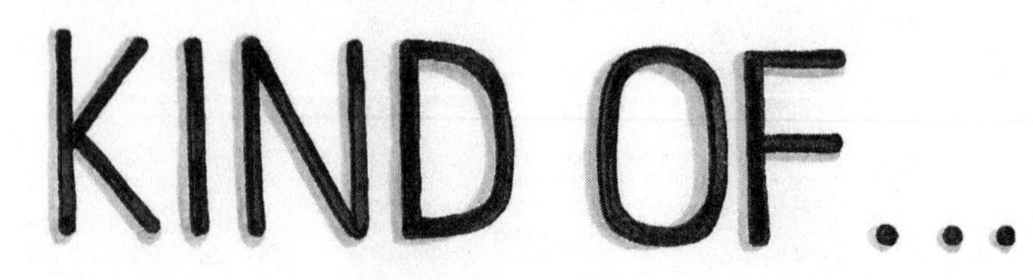
KIND OF...

CRAFT
CORNER

There's even a camp dog!

From what we all heard, Outdoor School was the best part of the whole year.

Aside from a trip advisor, some camp staffers, and a handful of high school volunteers, we'd be on our own—

away from EVERYTHING for

In middle school years, that was practically a LIFETIME!

The longest field trip we ever had in elementary school was our visit to the aquarium . . .

but that only ended up going overnight because our bus broke down.

THIS was different.

This was something else entirely . . .

DOM.

The news of Outdoor School couldn't have come at a better time. Sometimes, I felt like middle school was just a gigantic hamster wheel that never stopped spinning.

Every day was the same.

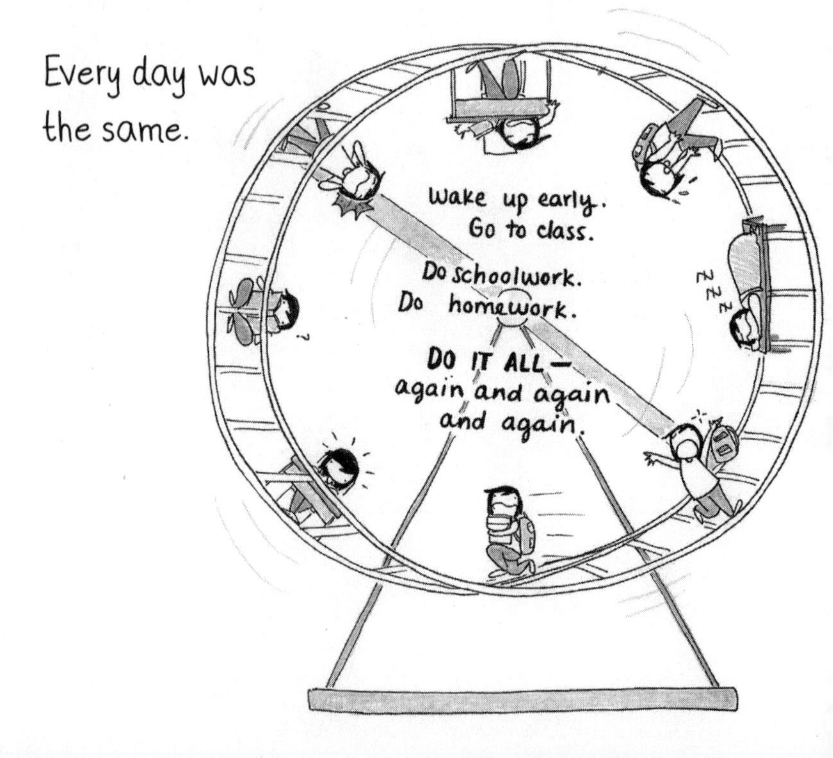

Wake up early.
Go to class.
Do schoolwork.
Do homework.
DO IT ALL—
again and again
and again.

It seemed like nothing would ever change, and we were just stuck in the same old routine. I had been starting to feel like a zombie lately—or maybe more like a zombie hamster trapped in the endless cycle of Pointdexter Middle School life.

But I wasn't sure what to do about it.

I wasn't the only one, either.

We ALL felt it happening—

We were basically becoming a class full of undead students.

I guess, in their own way, zombies are kind of stuck in the Middles too, so maybe we actually had some things in common.

But once the news about Outdoor School came out, everything changed. In the weeks leading up to the trip, it was all anyone could talk about!

The thought of escaping our normal lives—even just for a bit—was enough to bring us all back from the dead.

I couldn't help but get excited too.

Plus, I needed a serious break from my family.

The Wu household was in a particularly EXTREME state of madness lately.

Mom had just started one of her intense decluttering phases, and it always took at least a week for things to get back to normal.

To add to the chaos, Clara had recently seen an online video of a skateboarding dog and was determined to re-create it.

Mr. Felix McSnuggles the Third seemed significantly less determined.

On top of that, Aunt Lisa was staying with us while her home was being fumigated, so the house felt more crowded than usual.

Of course, even at Outdoor School, I couldn't escape my family entirely.

Peter was one of the high school camp counselors this year.

I knew what THAT meant.

Mom seemed to think that having him there would be a good thing. She probably figured I couldn't handle being on my own, but I'd prove her wrong.

This trip would be the longest I'd ever been away from home, but I actually wasn't that worried about it.

Maxine, Logan, and Jess would be with me, and I was pretty sure that . . .

Still, the night before the trip, I couldn't help but feel a little nervous.

That's when I got

The jitters weren't necessarily BAD, but they weren't great either. They always showed up at the worst possible time and took up too much space.

Plus, you could never get rid of them when you wanted to.

Every time I'd come close to falling asleep, another thought would wriggle loose and start bouncing around.

I managed to sleep eventually, but when I woke up, they were still there.

I thought they would
NEVER go away. . . .

But as soon as we pulled into the parking lot and saw everyone gathering outside, I started getting less nervous and more

So I didn't notice them as much.

Once we got to school, we were supposed to check in with Mrs. Lopez, this year's Outdoor School trip advisor. Most of us knew Mrs. Lopez as the school librarian, so at first, it was hard to even imagine her surviving in the wilderness—

until we found out that she used to be a pretty famous rock climber when she was younger.

Who knew?

Mrs. Lopez may have been prepared for the outdoors, but nothing could've prepared her for the horde of parents she was facing that morning.

Thankfully, Mom played it cool. Probably because Peter was there with me or because she just didn't feel like getting out of the car. Or both.

When we said good-bye, it actually hit me that I wouldn't be home for an entire week, but I didn't want anyone to think I couldn't handle it, so I tried to play it cool too.

Before she drove away, she gave us one of those classically sentimental Mom looks and said,

As soon as she was gone, I went off to find my friends in the crowd and left Peter to do whatever it was a volunteer camp counselor was supposed to do.

Everyone said Outdoor School was going to be an unforgettable experience, but last time I checked, they didn't have an annoyingly popular older brother as their chaperone.

I didn't need him to look out for me, and I was going to prove it!

The only problem was, there was so much happening around the bus loop that I didn't really know where to start.

I couldn't seem to find my friends anywhere. . . .

And by the time I looked back,
I had lost sight of Peter too.

Just when I was starting
to get really worried,
I heard someone
call my name
ABBIE!
and turned around to see
SYDNEY
PARK.

She and Peter had been friends
for FOREVER, though I wasn't sure why.
Sydney was much cooler than my brother—
and she didn't flaunt it either.

She was the only one of his friends who I actually kind of liked. Maybe because she always treated me like a regular person and NOT like I was her friend's little sister.

When I was younger, I used to wish that she and Peter would magically switch places so I could have a fun older sister instead.

Once I explained the situation to her,

she knew exactly what to do.

Before I knew it, we had dropped off all my stuff, checked in, and found Maxine, Logan, and Jess.

If only I had grown up
with HER instead. . . .

When the first bus pulled into the bus loop, I couldn't believe it! This was no ordinary bus—it was a COACH bus.

It was NOTHING like the beat-up, boring yellow school buses we usually got.

Up until that point, Outdoor School was just some distant idea, but now it finally hit me—

CHAPTER THREE

Once all the buses arrived, Mrs. Lopez started separating us into groups and ushering everyone on board.

Maxine, Logan, Jess, and I made sure to stick together so we wouldn't get separated.

The bus was NOT something any of us wanted to face alone—

even if it WAS a fancy coach bus.

We originally wanted to sit in the back, because everyone said the back was the best place to sit, but Peter and his friends had already taken over!

OF COURSE I ended up on the same bus as Peter. OF COURSE.

I wasn't thrilled about sharing a bus with my older brother, but everyone else seemed to LOVE it.

Everyone seemed to love HIM.

I knew he didn't plan it like that, but whether Peter meant to or not, he always had a way of overshadowing me.

This was THE CURSE OF THE MIDDLE WU.

I didn't want it to follow me to Outdoor School too. . . .

Not that I had much of a choice.

We were so different, it was hard to believe we were even related.
PETER moved through the world with an annoying sense of certainty.
Nothing scared him.
OF COURSE NOT.
Everything came easily to him.
No matter where he was or who he was with...
he BELONGED.

At least, everyone else seemed to think so.
Personally, I didn't see it.

As soon as Peter and his friends started telling stories about their time at Outdoor School, they had the entire bus hanging on their every word.

I couldn't help but overhear.

Up until now, I had thought of this trip as a temporary escape from middle school, but maybe it can be more than that.

Outdoor School is what YOU make it...
It's the best!
Legends are born!
Legacies are built!
Anything can happen!

I had to admit . . .

their stories were pretty epic.

ARH-WOOooooo...
ARH-WOOoooooo!
oh!
hehehe!
camp dog
la la la
la la la
la la la la
la la
OOH!

AHHHHHHH LAKE MONSTER!!!
MWAHAHAHAHA
WOAH
OMG
AHH
DANG
COOL

I had no clue what this week had in store for us, but I guess that was the point.

It was kind of exciting
and scary at the same time.

The uncertainty of it brought back those weird jitters, but they didn't bother me as much this time around.

Maybe I was getting used to them.

The farther we got from Pointdexter Middle School, the more I started to think that maybe this was what I needed.

Maybe this would be
an adventure
after all!

CHAPTER
FOUR

When we stepped off the bus, it felt like we were stepping into another world.

EVERYTHING WAS
DIFFERENT.

It was quiet in a
calm sort of way.

There was so much green.

It smelled better here,
like the pine-fresh smell
of cleaning supplies
or air freshener—
only REAL.

Too bad I only got to enjoy it for eleven
minutes and twenty-seven seconds.

As soon as we unloaded all our stuff from the bus, Mrs. Lopez decided to drop the biggest nightmare of a bomb . . .

I hadn't even considered a scenario where I wasn't in the same cabin as at least one of my friends. . . .

But turns out, we were ALL SPLIT UP.

Maybe this was Mrs. Lopez's revenge for that one time I snuck snacks into the library and got crumbs all over the reading carpet.

It was bad enough that we were separated, but it got even worse when I found out who was in MY group.

My cabin counselor was this girl named

Katrina.

Unlike a lot of the other
high school volunteers,
she didn't seem all that
excited to be there. In fact,
she didn't seem to care at all.

On the other hand, the girls in my cabin
were EXTRA excited to be there.

The only problem was, they knew
each other already . . .

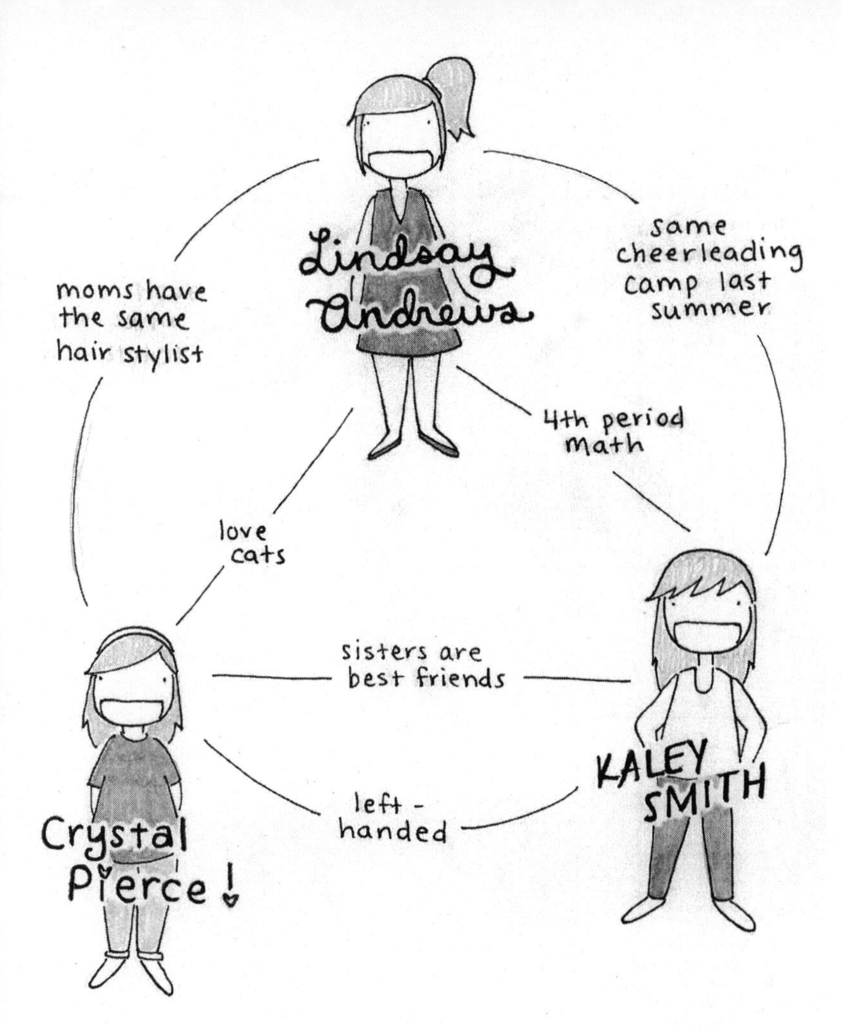

and they weren't particularly interested in getting to know me.

Plus, they clicked with each other in a way that I just DIDN'T.

Once Mrs. Lopez finished reading off the whole list of names, everyone started heading to their cabins to unpack.

On the way there, Katrina barely paid attention to where we were going . . .

while Crystal, Lindsay, and Kaley just talked to each other the whole time.

I had no idea what they were talking about and I couldn't think of anything to say to them, but they didn't seem to notice one way or the other.

It's like they forgot I was even there.

When we finally made it to our cabin, things didn't get much better.

They already had their beds picked out, so I got stuck on the bottom bunk with the lumpy mattress and the weird sweat stains.

I tried to tell myself that it didn't REALLY matter. I wasn't planning on spending that much time in the cabin anyway. There was plenty of stuff to do outside.

Plus, I had Maxine, Logan, and Jess. . . .

That night, everyone gathered in

for our official "Welcome to Outdoor School" orientation session.

Despite its intense name, the Arena was actually just this outdoor amphitheater big enough to fit everyone at camp.

We were forced to sit with our cabins for "bonding" purposes, which felt a little excessive. We already had to share a bathroom and sleep in the same room. How much bonding time did we need?

It was a pretty standard "welcome" orientation—laying out the camp rules, introducing all the counselors and staff, encouraging us to "make the most of our time" and all that.

But then, Mrs. Lopez brought up . . .

THE
GOL

DEN PIG!

The Golden Pig wasn't a REAL pig. It was a metal figurine about as big as an average-size burger.

I'm pretty sure it was just spray-painted gold, but that didn't matter because it was LEGENDARY.

The Golden Pig was the heart of Outdoor School and the center of a historic camp competition.

The mission was simple.

PROTECT THE GOLDEN PIG.

RULES!

① Someone must be in charge of the Golden Pig at all times.

② The Golden Pig must always be visible. It cannot be hidden!

③ Every time the camp bell rings, the Golden Pig must be passed to another person.

DO NOT, UNDER ANY CIRCUMSTANCES, LET THE COUNSELORS TAKE THE GOLDEN PIG.

The entire week was
an epic clash of

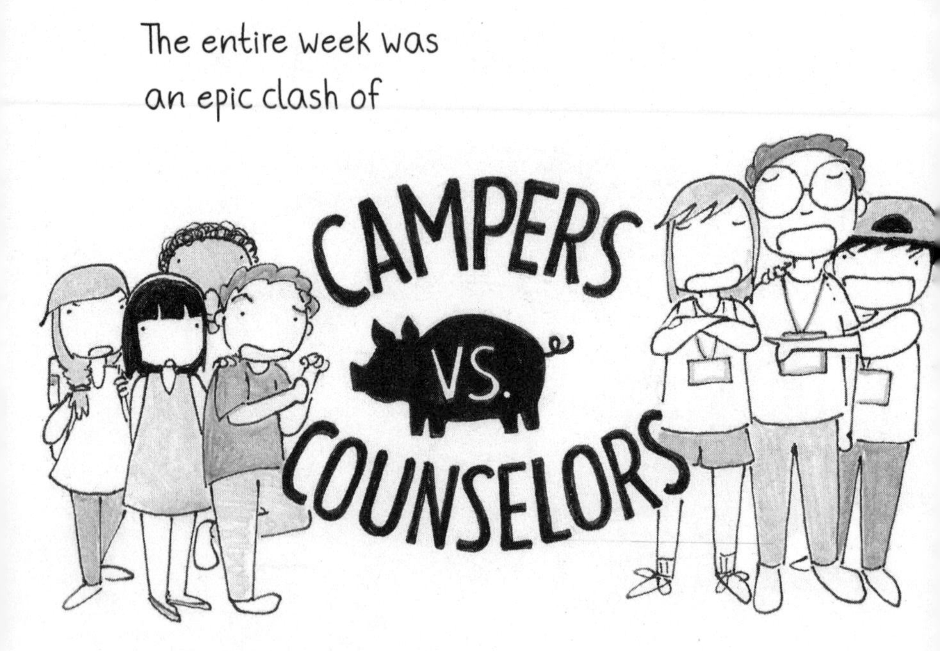

culminating in one
very important question
at the end of camp—

WHO
HAD THE
GOLDEN PIG?

This Outdoor School camp tradition had been going on since the beginning of time . . . or at least as long as Outdoor School had been around.

In all the years that Outdoor School and the Golden Pig had existed, the campers had NEVER WON.

The closest they got was Peter's year. They were only a few hours away from victory, but then . . .

Some people called it a curse, and maybe it was. . . . But curses could be broken, and this year HAD to be different.

If we could do it . . .

if we could keep
the Golden Pig
away from our
camp counselors . . .

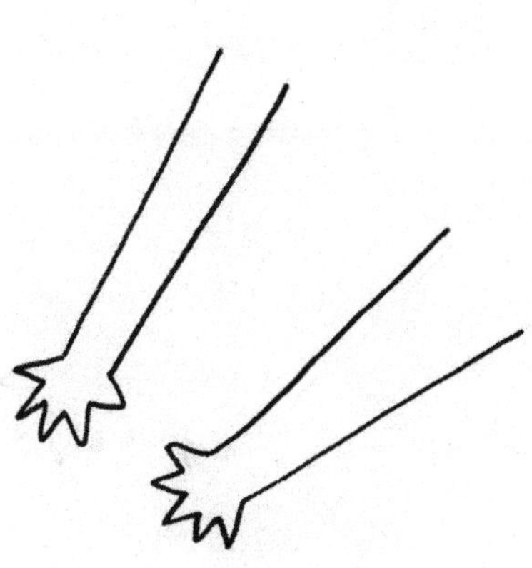

if we could break
this seemingly
unbreakable
losing streak . . .

we would go down in Outdoor School
history as LEGENDS. Not to mention,
we'd be immortalized on . . .

The Wall was a sacred space in the center of camp—one side dedicated to the counselors who were able to steal the Golden Pig, and the other side reserved for the campers who managed to protect it.

Our side was empty.

. . . but not for long.
This was OUR year.

THIS COULD
BE OUR
LEGACY.

Plus, rumor had it that the winning side got a massive victory party with pizza and cake and ice cream floats, while the losing side had to take care of all the end-of-camp cleanup.

We had to win no matter what.

CHAPTER FIVE

Besides protecting the Golden Pig, there was a lot happening at Outdoor School. The camp was so big that it took us a while to figure out our way around,

but once we did, it felt like a whole new world was open to us.

Life at Outdoor School was NOTHING like what we were used to at Pointdexter.

Instead of an annoying, high-pitched bell going off every few hours, the camp speakers played a series of pleasant, melodic chimes to keep us on schedule.

Our classes weren't typical math or history classes, and half the time, they didn't even happen in a classroom!

Then there was the *food*.

The dining hall at camp was the complete opposite of the cafeteria at school. The kitchen staff always had snacks for us, and their food was actually GOOD.

The best part, though, was

Everything that made Outdoor School different from Pointdexter was great, but it also made things

And NOT in a good way.

I had always known that my friends and I were very different . . . but being different kind of worked for us. Istvan always said that we only had one thing in common:

HOW
MUCH
WE
LOVED
PASTRIES

. . . which honestly seemed like a pretty legitimate basis for friendship to me.

I guess I just thought that, like everything else, we would go through Outdoor School together. . . .

But when it came down to it, they each had REALLY different ideas of how to use their time there.

Jess planned to go on all these intense hiking expeditions. . . .

Logan wanted to check out this exclusive board game society that he heard about from one of the counselors. . . .

And I think Maxine liked the idea of just hanging out with the other girls in her cabin.

Before I knew what had happened, it was decided. We would each do our own thing and meet up

—whatever THAT meant.

While they all had different things to do and different people to do them with,

I didn't know where to go. I wasn't sure I fit in anywhere.

What made it worse was that, no matter where I went, I kept running into Peter.

I thought about my current predicament and how this would NEVER happen to him.

Eventually, I just went back to my cabin—not that I really had a place there either.

The girls in my cabin weren't bad in any obvious way. They didn't play pranks on me or take my stuff or say mean things.

They just didn't seem to want me there.

And that sort of felt worse.

When "later" finally rolled around and we all reunited in the dining hall for dinner, something felt off in a way that it hadn't before.

Was it because we were at Outdoor School?

Or was it US?

Maxine, Logan, and Jess
didn't seem to notice. . . .

So I wondered if
it was just ME . . .

and that DEFINITELY made it worse.

In situations like this, it was good to try to get another point of view, but that was much easier to do at home.

Aunt Lisa was my go-to counsel for most things, and Istvan always had wise stuff to say about life.

Then there was Mom, who gave pretty good advice when you needed it. Even Clara provided unexpected insight every now and then.

Out here, I wasn't sure *who* to go to.

Well . . . I guess that wasn't entirely true.

But I couldn't bring myself to ask Peter—especially not after I *swore* I wouldn't need his help.

Besides, what would Peter know about something like this? He NEVER had problems making friends or being included.

He wouldn't understand, and the thought of trying to explain it to him was just too embarrassing.

I'd NEVER live it down.
But... maybe I wouldn't have to.

Peter wasn't the only person I knew here.

Sydney was just as smart as Peter and probably a lot easier to talk to about this sort of thing.

In fact, Sydney was maybe the PERFECT person to ask for advice.

She was bold in a way that most people weren't . . . in a way that I definitely wasn't.

She wasn't afraid to say what she thought, and when she talked, people didn't just hear what she had to say—they *listened*.

Plus, she was one of the few people who didn't mind putting Peter in his place.

How could I not respect the advice of someone who knew how to keep my brother's ego in check?

It wasn't just that, though. She was different from the other high school camp counselors.

I felt like I could trust her. Like she wouldn't laugh at me or think I was being silly or write me off.

When I finally managed to get her alone, I wasn't sure where to start, but as soon as she asked,

it all just started coming out of me.

Sydney didn't respond at first, and my immediate thought was that I had made a HUGE mistake.

I shouldn't have said anything.
I shouldn't have felt this way.
I had gone too far. I had said too much.
I was being ridiculous.
I was being a baby.
It wasn't a big deal.

But then . . .

HMM...
well, I remember being LOST when I first got here too.
This place is like a DIFFERENT WORLD.
THAT'S THE POINT, THOUGH.
HERE you can try ANYTHING.
EVERYTHING.
Especially NEW THINGS you're not used to.

OUTDOOR SCHOOL IS your chance TO
DO — whatever YOU want. BE — whoever YOU want.
YOU HAVE TO JUST GO FOR IT.
You NEVER KNOW WHAT can happen!
You might even FIND OUT STUFF about YOURSELF that you didn't know before.

Sydney was probably right. Everything she said actually made sense—well, except for that part about finding out new stuff about myself.

I KNEW MYSELF.

DIDN'T I?

I mean, what could I NOT know?

UNLESS . . .

Could there be another version of me that I *didn't* know yet? A better version?

Mom always said that I should try to be the BEST version of myself.

Maybe, at Outdoor School, I could be. Maybe this was my chance.

CHAPTER
SEVEN

The only problem was, Sydney made it sound so easy, like it was just a matter of saying yes to things.

of course
yes
DEFINITELY
why not
i'm in
YUP
OKAY
SURE
totally
CERTAINLY
OKIE DOKIE
sounds good

But that was only part of it.

Everyone else had found their own unique place at Outdoor School.

But where was I in all that?

Their new friends were so *different*—
from each other and from me.

I wasn't sure I could fit in with any of them.

I knew I was supposed to just enjoy myself and not think too much about getting them to like me, but if I was really honest about it,

I *WANTED* THEM TO.

I wanted to be able to walk into a room and trust that I was *wanted* there.

Didn't everyone?

It was times like this when I wished I was *already* Abbie 2.0.

ABBIE 2.0
faced the world
with an unshakable
sense of confidence.
Nothing fazed her.
OBVIOUSLY.
She could handle anything.
No matter where she was or who she was with...
she FIT IN.

At least, I *wanted* her to be.

I might not have been Abbie 2.0 yet, but I had to try my best. The first step was to figure out my place at Outdoor School by trying more things.

This also meant expanding the idea of what I was used to and ignoring some of my most basic instincts.

When Jess and her friends invited me to hike Dead Man's Point with them, I thought about how . . .

- I was NOT a particularly good hiker.
- Nature could be *very* unforgiving.
- As a personal rule, I tried to avoid places associated with the word "DEAD."

BUT I had never really given outdoor activities much of a chance before, so I said,

When Maxine asked if I wanted to hang out with her cabinmates one afternoon, I thought about how . . .

- They were pretty popular at school and I was pretty obviously *not*.
- The girls in my OWN cabin didn't seem to like me very much.
- I wasn't really sure what "hanging out" actually meant.

BUT we weren't at school anymore, and there was a possibility we might actually get along, so I said,

When Logan wanted me to join his team for this massive board game tournament, I thought about how . . .

- Being on a team was a LOT of pressure.
- Logan and his buddies were *very* competitive.
- My general strategy in gaming (and life) was to just survive as long as possible—not necessarily "win."

BUT I liked games, and if there was ever a time to challenge myself, this was probably it, so I said,

I wasn't sure if things would work out,

After a while, I wasn't even thinking about *trying* to say YES to things.

I just *did* because they seemed fun.

I thought that, eventually, I would figure out exactly what I was supposed to be doing at Outdoor School—but it wasn't that simple.

Turns out, I actually *liked* all the things I thought I wouldn't. I even got along with everyone!

Something had changed, but I wasn't sure what.

It HAD to be because we were at Outdoor School. Sydney was right when she said it was a totally different world.

At Outdoor School, I felt like I could be something more than myself . . . a new, improved me.

And I liked it.

The more time I spent there, the more it felt like I had fallen through some kind of hole in the Universe.

Each day was totally different depending on who I spent it with and what we were doing.

Sometimes, it felt like we were at completely different Outdoor Schools—
each one existing in entirely
different
dimensions.

The only constant was the Golden Pig and our shared determination to keep it safe.

There had been a few minor incidents—

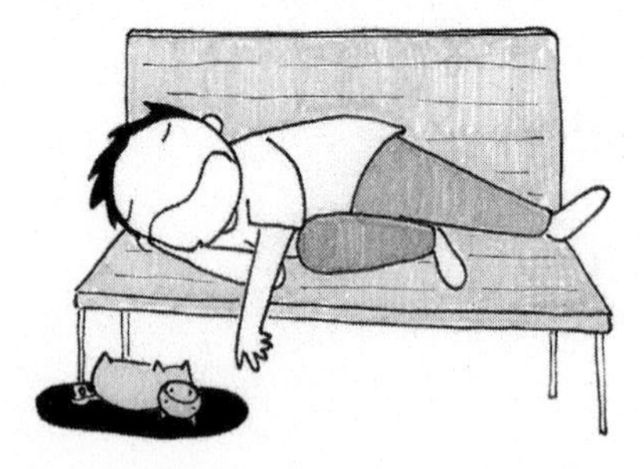

like when Ed Tran's post-lunch nap left the Pig practically defenseless . . .

or Hayley Parks's flirting almost cost us the game.

And then there was the whole lake debacle. . . .

But despite all the close calls, the Golden Pig was still OURS.

Not many campers had ever protected it for THIS long before.

Soon, we'd be making camp history . . .

and the counselors were NOT happy about it.

It was hard to believe that we were over halfway through our week at Outdoor School.

One minute, it felt slowed down and stretched out, like we'd been away at camp for ages. Then the next minute, it was as if everything was in hyper-speed and it was all about to end before I could even catch up.

For most people, the fact that Outdoor School was almost over meant we were that much closer to winning the Golden Pig and breaking the curse. . . .

To me, it meant we'd go back to our normal middle school lives, and everything would return to the way it was before.

BUT I WASN'T READY FOR THAT YET.

The truth is, time wasn't the only thing that was different at Outdoor School.

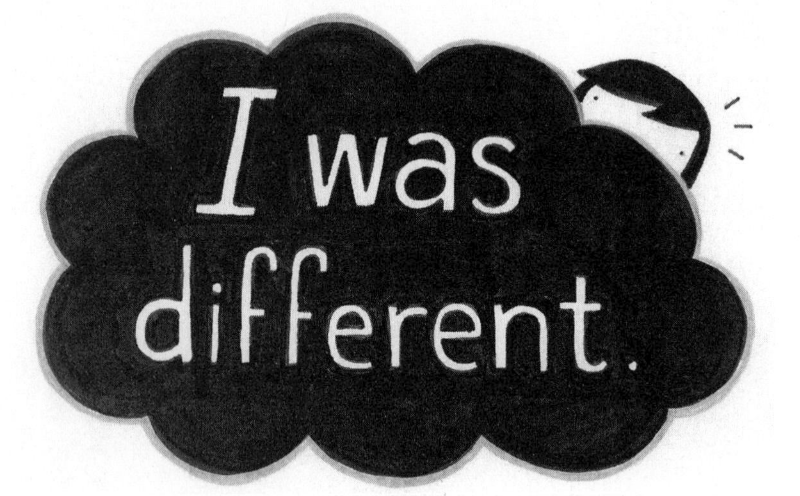

I did things that I never thought I would (or could).

I was braver
and bolder than
I usually was.
and I-I-I-I
will always
love you-u-u
I somehow felt
smarter and more
interesting too.
HA
HA
HA
HA
HA
HA
HA
HA
HA
HA
HA
HA
HA
HA
HA
HA

Here, I was

Back home, I was just plain Abbie Wu.

But there was nothing I could do to stop Outdoor School from ending . . . aside from inventing some kind of interdimensional time machine,

and that just seemed like a LOT of work.

So I decided to try to make the most of the time I had left. . . .

DO ALL THE THINGS I'D WANTED TO DO HERE,
HANG OUT WITH ALL THE PEOPLE I'D GOTTEN TO KNOW AT CAMP,
ENJOY ALL THE STUFF I'D MISS ONCE LIFE WENT BACK TO NORMAL.

It seemed like a lot, but I told myself it was just a matter of balance.

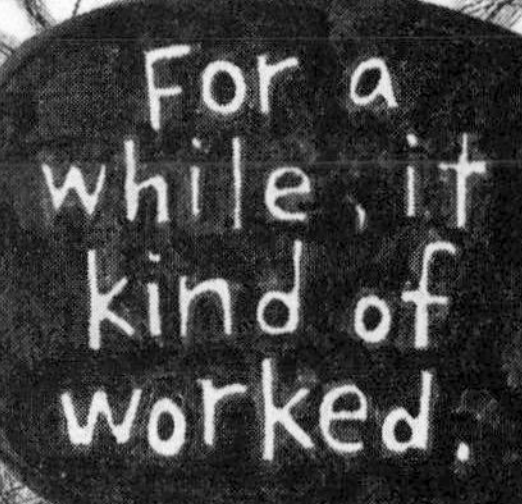
For a while, it kind of worked.
But then things began to blend together.

I was so busy trying not to miss out on everything...
that I started to lose track of why I was doing ANYTHING.

Maybe I was taking on too much, but I didn't want to give any of it up.

Admitting I couldn't handle things was not an option either, so I just tried to play it cool.

That seemed like the evolved, Abbie 2.0 thing to do.

Peter was the only person who questioned it.

I made up some fake excuse about eating too many s'mores. He seemed to buy it, which just proved that Peter really didn't know as much as he thought he did.

But, in a way, he was right.

Things WERE off. I just couldn't see it until it was TOO LATE.

There was a definite hierarchy when it came to bad things happening to you.

Some bad things were completely out of your control—stuff like earthquakes and hurricanes and being born a middle child.

Then there were situational bad things that happened because you were in the wrong place at the wrong time . . .

or because someone was out to get you . . .

not to mention things that were the result of just plain bad luck.

But that was nothing compared to the *worst* kind of bad thing . . .

THE KIND YOU SHOULD HAVE SEEN COMING.

Maybe if you had, you could have stopped it—

BUT YOU DIDN'T.

Which made it

ALL YOUR FAULT.

Which made it

WORSE.

THAT was

THE ULTIMATE
LOWEST
totally
UNFORGIVABLE
absolute
WORST
BAD THING.

And THAT was the sort of bad thing that happened to me in our last few days at Outdoor School.

I called it

THE INCIDENT.

In retrospect, the events leading up to it were just a series of minor bad things foreshadowing something MUCH worse.

The day before IT happened, Alexis Bunker found me and handed over the Golden Pig.

Being the Keeper of the Golden Pig was supposed to be an honor. . . .

But I couldn't help but see it as just ANOTHER thing to keep track of.

Life at Outdoor School had already gotten way more complicated than I expected.

I should have known it was just a matter of time before I slipped and everything fell apart.

* It happened at **BREAKFAST**.

I remember that part clearly because, like most people, the morning was when I was least functional . . . and therefore most vulnerable to bad things.

The first bad thing was that I was LATE.

Context was important, so it should be noted that the day before THE INCIDENT had been a VERY full day.

Between ziplining through the forest that morning,

launching a prank war
on an unsuspecting
boys' cabin
after lunch,

and spending most of the
night huddled around
a very intense
board game . . .

I WAS *EXHAUSTED*.

So exhausted, in fact, that I
slept right through my alarm. . . .

Which brought us to the morning of
THE INCIDENT.

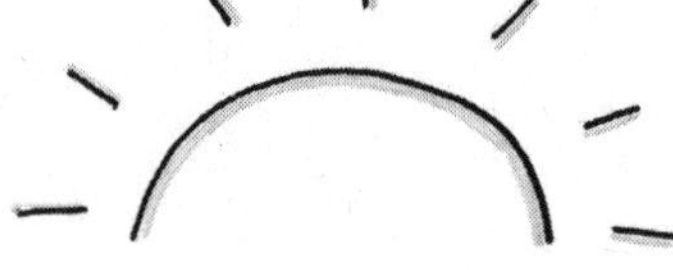

Not only did the other girls in my cabin
leave for breakfast without me,
they left without bothering
to wake me up.

And on cinnamon
roll day, of all days!

Even though I was already late, I was
determined to make it to breakfast before
the kitchen ran out.

I brushed my teeth in record time but got stuck when it came to deciding what to wear.

I couldn't remember what I was doing that day, let alone what outfit I needed. Everything was jumbled and I didn't have time to figure it out.

On top of all that, I couldn't find a clean pair of socks, so I ended up going to breakfast *totally* mismatched.

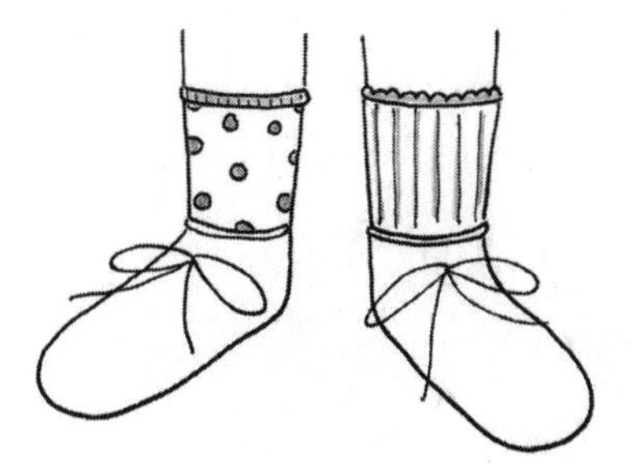

At least I managed to grab the last cinnamon roll— not that it mattered much.

Just as I went to take a bite, I heard the counselors cheering, and the whole place erupted into chaos.

I wasn't sure why, and I didn't think much of it . . . that is, until Alexis came over to me in a panic—

Abbie, WHERE'S THE GOLDEN PIG?

AND THAT'S WHEN I KNEW...

4
...
?
!
MWAHAHA
AHAHAH
HAHAHA
AHAAH
I HAD DONE A
very, very, very
BAD THING.

I couldn't face anyone after that. I couldn't even finish the rest of my cinnamon roll.

Talk about *tragic*.

If I hadn't been rushing to make it to breakfast before the cinnamon rolls ran out, I would've remembered the Golden Pig. Then none of this would've happened.

How ironic that *this* was my downfall—betrayed by a PASTRY!

I wanted to blame it for everything . . .

or the kitchen for not baking enough cinnamon rolls

or my cabinmates for not waking me up

or my mom for not reminding me to pack more socks

or even the camp for scheduling breakfast WAY too early.

But in reality, I knew it was ME.

After THE INCIDENT, things were different.

I felt distant from everyone at camp in a way that I hadn't before. Protecting the Golden Pig had been the one thing that brought us all together—and I had RUINED it.

That night by the bonfire, I overheard some other campers talking about the Golden Pig. . . .

It gave me a heavy feeling in my chest that I just couldn't shake.

After that, I didn't know how to be around them without feeling like I would just ruin things.

WAS I CURSED?
WAS I *THE CURSE*?

My marshmallows kept catching fire, and I took that as a sign.

I had been so caught up in being this better version of myself—

the version that was a part of everything, that everyone liked, that could handle anything.

But Abbie 2.0 would NEVER have lost the Golden Pig.

Maybe the reality was that
there was no Abbie 2.0—

And that didn't seem good enough.

Even though no one said anything, I could tell that they all *thought* it. Who could blame them?

Maxine, Logan, and Jess
tried to make me feel better . . .

but it was useless.

Before all this, I felt included in everything. But after THE INCIDENT, I couldn't bring myself to be a part of any of it.

It was better for everyone if I stayed out of the way and did things on my own. . . .

Except THAT turned out to be harder than I thought.

And, honestly, it just wasn't as *fun*.

For a while, I steered clear of pretty much everyone at camp.

Then, as I was playing a game of chess against myself, Sydney stopped by to see how I was doing.

She could tell that things weren't great.

This time, there was nothing Sydney could say or do to make this better, but I guess she still wanted to try.

I think I know what you need.
WAIT HERE...

After a few minutes, she came back . . .

with PETER.

Before I knew it, she had left the two of us alone together.

WHAT WAS SHE THINKING?!?!

There was no way talking to Peter would solve anything. He couldn't possibly understand what I was going through.

At least, that's what I THOUGHT until he sat down and started talking.

SO, YOU KNOW HOW WE LOST THE GOLDEN PIG THE YEAR I WAS HERE AT OUTDOOR SCHOOL?

well...
IT WAS ME.
I LOST THE
golden pig

I couldn't believe it.

I just assumed the person responsible for losing the Golden Pig was branded a social pariah and shipped off to Siberia (metaphorically, of course) until the end of time or, at the very least, until the end of middle school.

But I guess not.

"It's not the end of the world."

He must have gotten
that from Mom.

It was one of her most *popular* phrases.

I used to hate when she said it, because even
if the world wasn't *technically* going to end,
it sure felt like it was to ME.

But for some reason, there was something familiar and unexpectedly comforting about hearing it now.

It actually DID make me feel better.

Losing the Golden Pig (and knowing that Peter had lost it too) connected us in a way that I hadn't expected.

I always thought that Peter didn't really know me, but maybe the truth was that I didn't really know HIM.

To me, he had always
been this annoyingly
perfect older brother
who was all the things
I wasn't.

It was strange to consider
that he, too, could be someone
who doubted himself
and made mistakes
and wasn't always
so *sure*.

And maybe,
in that way,
we weren't so
different after all.

So I decided I might as well tell him everything.
IT'S TOO MUCH!

Never in a million years would I have expected to spend time at Outdoor School talking to my BROTHER.

We didn't just talk about Outdoor School or the Golden Pig either.

We talked about . . .

how Katrina had hated him ever since he beat her in their fifth-grade spelling bee,

how seeing Mom and Aunt Lisa bickering reminded him of Clara and me,

and how Mr. Felix McSnuggles the Third clearly resented having a kitty stage mom.

I learned . . .

that he became friends with Sydney by accident,

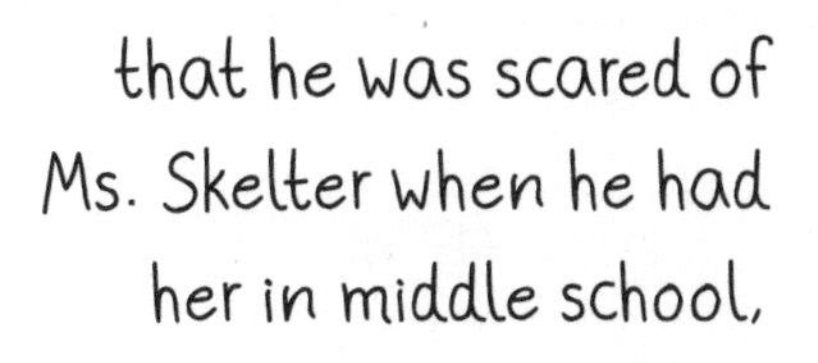

that he was scared of Ms. Skelter when he had her in middle school,

and that he didn't really like the Spencer sisters either.

Eventually, we got around to talking about me and what I should do with the rest of my time at Outdoor School.

For once, I wish he had just told me what I needed to do. That would have been so much easier.

Instead, he said something that stuck in my head for the rest of the day.

You're ABBIE WU.
You'll figure it out.

It never felt like that to me. But he genuinely seemed to believe it, and that was enough to make me want to believe it too.

After talking to Peter, I knew I couldn't just keep running away from people or wallowing in my feelings. I didn't want to end Outdoor School like that.

I had to face what had happened and try to make things RIGHT.

But HOW?

I thought about it a lot, and no matter what, I kept coming back to the Golden Pig.

I couldn't take back the fact that I had lost it in the first place . . .

. . . BUT WHAT WAS STOPPING ME FROM TAKING IT BACK—*literally*?
!

There weren't any rules against that, and ultimately, what really mattered was who had the Golden Pig at the end of camp.

IT HAD TO BE ME.

This could be my epic
redemption—
Hooray!
Abbie is the best!
Wow!
She did it!

returning the Golden Pig to the campers and proving my worth to everyone at Outdoor School.

Why did we ever doubt her?

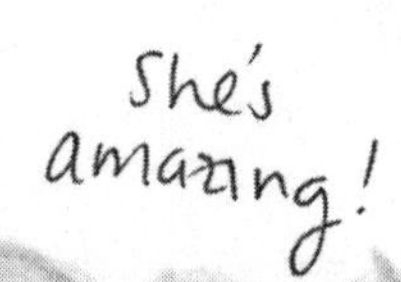

There was just one thing standing in my way. Well, a group of things.

The counselors were VERY protective of the Golden Pig. Wherever the Pig was, there were at least two or three counselors by its side.

It was almost impossible to get close to it. No matter what strategy I tried, they managed to block it.

Nothing seemed to work. At this rate, I'd never be able to get it back on my own.

Taking back the Golden Pig was NOT going to be easy.

If I really wanted to make things right, I needed help . . .

Despite all our differences, every camper wanted the same thing. The Golden Pig brought us all together before THE INCIDENT, so maybe bringing us together was how we would get it back!

I decided to call an urgent, top secret, campers-only meeting.

I wasn't sure if anyone would show up,

TOP SECRET MEETING!!!
campers only
6:30
pass it on.

but a lot of
them did.
Even the girls
from my cabin!

When I told them what
I wanted to do—

Listen—
I'M GOING
TO
get it back
... BUT
I CAN'T
do it
ALONE.

what I wanted
US to do—

I NEED you—
all
OF YOU.

they listened.

More than that . . .

WE can MAKE THIS HAPPEN.
WE can BREAK THE CURSE.
WE can TAKE BACK
the
golden pig.

they wanted to JOIN me.

TOGETHER!

It didn't just feel like redemption.

It felt like something I think I liked much better—

Outdoor School was almost over, so we didn't have much time to figure out how to take back the Golden Pig.

I wasn't completely sure how we were going to do it, but a bunch of people trying to figure it out together was a lot better than me trying to figure it out on my own.

At the same time, getting a bunch of very different people to do something together was NOT a simple task.

Even though we all wanted to get the Golden Pig back, we couldn't seem to agree on *how* to do it.

Were we all too different to make this work?

For a while, it seemed like we'd never get it together, and I felt torn between my friends all over again.

But then I remembered what Peter said.

I WAS
ABBIE WU.
I COULD
FIGURE
THIS OUT.

Sure, we all had different ideas of how to get the Golden Pig back, but that didn't have to be a *bad* thing.

In fact...

it could be EXACTLY what we needed to pull this off.

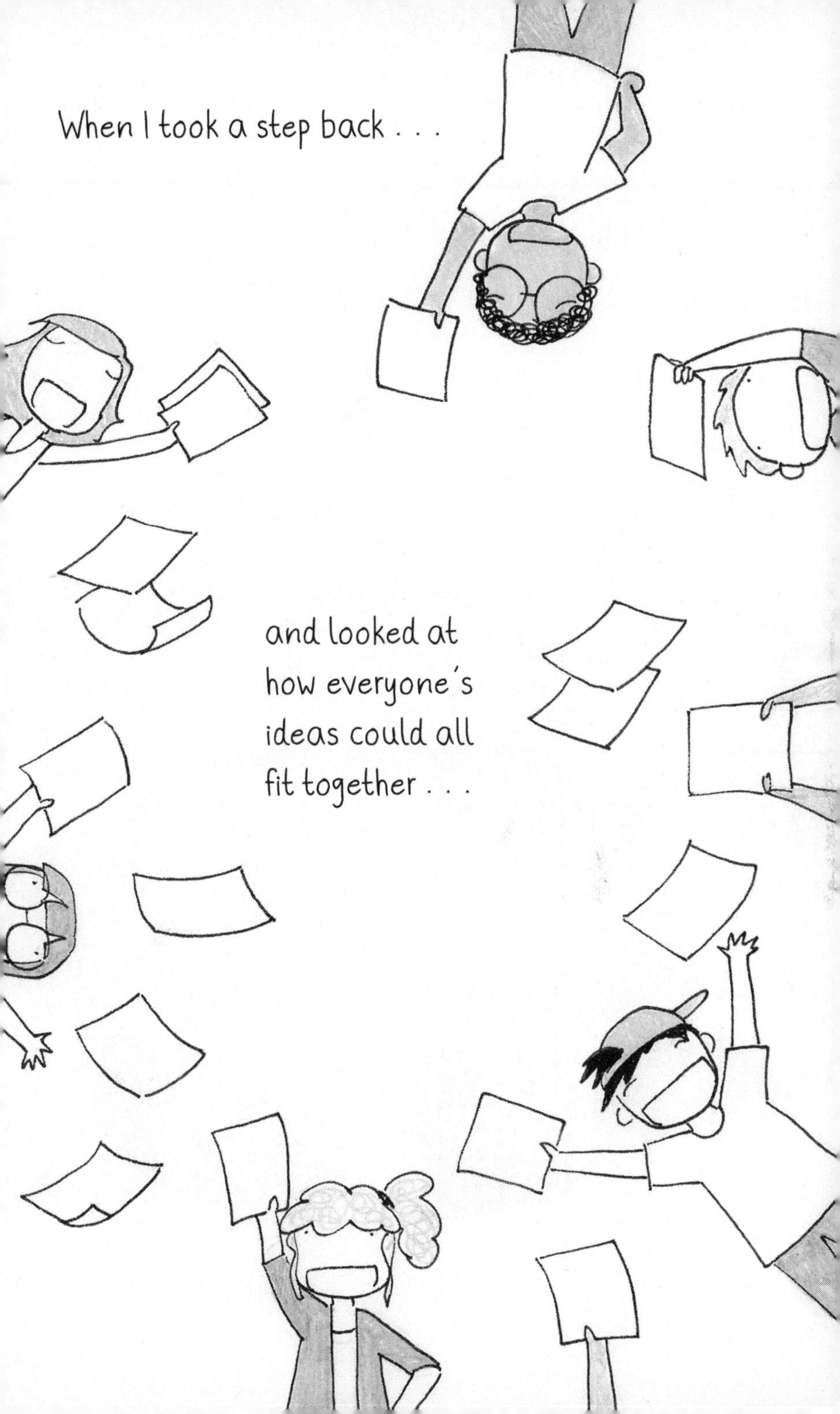
When I took a step back . . .
and looked at how everyone's ideas could all fit together . . .

MAP
IT JUST FELT...

RIGHT.

I had devised some pretty elaborate plans in my lifetime, but this one was different.

It wasn't just any plan—

No other group in the history of Outdoor School had ever come together to try something like this.

The way I saw it, this WAS our legacy.

Taking back the Golden Pig would
just make it more . . . *official*.

It all came down to the last day of camp.

When I woke up that morning, I knew something big was about to happen—

for better or for worse.

Everyone had a part to play. I was designated head of the Golden Pig rescue squad.

There was a very small window of opportunity to get the Pig before the final assembly, so everything had to go according to plan.

It was a lot of pressure, and along with that pressure came those all-too-familiar jitters.

Except this time, I wasn't the only one—

and THAT made a difference.

I actually felt

about whatever happened.

For the first time since I'd lost the Golden Pig, I was a part of something bigger than just me.

Maybe that was what I REALLY wanted anyway.

COMMENCE
MISSION: BRING HOME THE BACON
LOCATE THE GOLDEN PIG
IDENTIFY + ASSESS THREAT
AHHHHH
FOOD STORAGE
TARGET ISOLATED

DEPLOY DISTRACTION + DIVERSION TEAM
CAKE IN THE CAFETERIA!
CAFETERIA
GOLDEN PIG RESCUE SQUAD, GO!

WELL?
WHAT HAPPENED?
DID WE GET IT?

Congrats,
You did

campers!
it!

Everything after that was a blur. It was, after all, the last day of Outdoor School, and last days always moved too fast.

Between saying good-bye to the camp staff and packing up all our stuff, there wasn't time to process that it was over.

Of course, there was also our victory party, which was undoubtedly the most EPIC celebration I had ever witnessed . . .

Though apparently they threw the party for campers every year—even when they lost the Golden Pig.

So it was actually just more of an "end of Outdoor School" party, which felt slightly less epic.

It honestly didn't hit me that we were really leaving until I saw those fancy coach buses parked at the entrance of the camp.

The whole scene was so familiar, and yet . . .

On the ride home, Maxine, Logan, and I finally got to sit at the back of the bus.

I don't know if we took full advantage of it, though. Everyone was so exhausted at that point that most of the bus just fell asleep as soon as it started moving.

I couldn't stop thinking about what would happen when we got back home.

WOULD THINGS GO BACK TO THE WAY THEY WERE?

WOULD WE REMEMBER THE GOLDEN PIG?

WOULD WE EVEN THINK ABOUT CAMP AT ALL?

OR WOULD WE ACT LIKE IT NEVER HAPPENED?

I felt like I
was different

or at least
like I was
seeing things
differently.

So much had changed at Outdoor School.

I wondered if, once we got back into the cycle of middle school life, the whole thing would feel like some kind of dream.

I guess, even if it did, it was a pretty good dream.

After all, we were part of camp history now.

Outdoor School was over, but next year, when they talked about camp legends and shared stories about the Golden Pig, they'd remember us.

We had made our place there . . .

and that was pretty great to me.

It was dark by the time we arrived at Pointdexter. I hadn't realized how far away Outdoor School was from home.

As soon as we pulled into the school parking lot, everyone pressed up against the windows to try to look outside.

A crowd of parents swarmed the bus, and Mrs. Lopez had to use the loudspeakers to get control of them.

Once the doors opened, everyone scrambled off and the parking lot descended into absolute chaos.

How anyone managed to find their way through the madness was beyond me.

Peter and I tried to stick together at first, but we got separated by the huge pile of stuff they were unloading from the bus.

I found my bag, but I totally lost track of Peter!

Then I heard his voice behind me.

And when I turned around,
it wasn't just Peter—

it was the whole family.

In that moment, it felt like I was standing between two different worlds.

But it didn't bother me.

I had been afraid that coming home
meant leaving behind everything
that had happened.

But now I realized
I didn't have to.

Outdoor School was a part of me now.

Besides, it felt
good to be home.

And as much as I had changed, it was nice to know some things were still the same.

ACKNOWLEDGMENTS

People always ask me what *Frazzled* is about, which seems simple but isn't. For me, these books are about a lot of things, but this one in particular is really about finding your place in the world and, above all, finding your people. I'm so lucky that Abbie Wu and I have found ours—

My editor, Margaret Anastas, who believed in Abbie from the beginning and is one of my greatest champions. My agent, Steve Malk, who always has my back, and the incomparable Hannah, who always has his.

The rest of my HarperCollins Children's Books family, of course—

The irreplaceable Luana, who is always on top of things. Superb book designers Andrea and Amy, who help get all these ideas out of my brain and onto the page. Bethany and my meticulous copy editors, who make sure I make sense.

Ann and Team Middle Grade, my amazing marketing hype people. The wonderful sales team and all the lovely booksellers who have been keeping *Frazzled* on their shelves. Caroline, Aubrey, and the publicity team, you know you are my people and I appreciate you so. Patty and the School & Library crew, thank you for getting *Frazzled* into the hands of teachers and librarians . . . and thank you to those teachers and librarians who continue to share these books with so many young readers.

One of the best things about making children's books is belonging to a phenomenal community of writers, illustrators, and publishing friends that supports and challenges me. Kidlit rules! A special thanks to Tae Keller, for always reading my early drafts and assuring me that they are worth continuing.

In a book about friendships and finding your place in the world, it feels important to acknowledge the people who have been with me along the way . . . but there is not nearly enough space here to fit you all. I hope it's enough to say: friends, this book is for you. Thanks for all the laughs. To my family—no matter where I go or how far away I am, thank you for always being there and being home.

Finally, thank you to all the readers who found something in *Frazzled* and followed me and Abbie all the way to book three. I know I'm biased, but you're the best part of this whole thing.

Kamolpat Trangratapit

BOOKI VIVAT is the *New York Times* bestselling author of the Frazzled series. She has been doodling somewhat seriously since 2011 and not-so-seriously since childhood. She grew up in Southern California and graduated from the University of California, San Diego. She lives in Brooklyn, New York.

More books by BOOKI VIVAT!

Abbie Wu is always in crisis, but this time, she's guaranteed, without a doubt, 100% doomed!

HARPER
An Imprint of HarperCollins*Publishers*

www.harpercollinschildrens.com • www.shelfstuff.com